AF428544

NOTHING BUT THE TRUTH

BOOK TWO OF THE GLORY
HALLELUJUAH SERIES

WRITTEN AND ILLUSTRATED
BY
WANDA HOMEN

Dedicated to my husband
Donald Homen

He has read all my books and
critiqued them, and we are still married!

BOOKS BY WANDA HOMEN

ESPERANZA SERIES:
Chico
Esperanza Smith
Rosy Posy Big Fat Nosy
Rosy Goes Catholic
Queen of the Basura
Esperanza Means Hope
Breakup *

BUTTERCUP SERIES:
Buttercup
Buttercup Goes Camping
Buttercup and the Bully
Buttercup Has a Rival
A Buttercup Christmas

MARLEY SERIES:
Spooky Magic in S.F. *
Not Too Nice! *
Marley's Trick on Santa*
Breakup*

OTHERS:
I Hate Dogs*
The Mud Hole*
The Dare*
The Good Loser*
That Ghost in the Attic

STORIES IN VERSE:
Marked by asterisk: (*)

GLORY SERIES:
Glory Hallelujah
Nothing but the Truth

MINPINS SERIES::
Rescued
 Whatever Happened
To Chase?
Frieden
 Punkin Patch
Nickie No-No
 Nickie No-No Revised
 The Magic Mirror *
 Mini Loves to Bark*
 Minpins: King of the
Toys*
Two Minpins and a
Skunk*
 Who Am I? *
Fakes*

Contents:

PART ONE: CHILDHOOD DAYS:

PART TWO: TEENAGE YEARS

PART ONE

CHILDHOOD DAYS

A WORD FROM JULIE

My Grannie is amazing. She can tell you stories about her life that you hope can stay in your mind forever. I remember sitting on her lap at the age of four and listening to her fantastic tales. Some of them were even about me! One day, Grannie hugged me close to her as she smiled and told me about my birth in her typical fairy tale style.

First, Grannie tells me my story and then she tells me hers. Her story is much longer covering her life up to the age of seventeen.

GRANNIE'S STORY JUST FOR ME

Not so long ago, there was a couple who was very sad. They had been married for three years and their fondest dream had not come true.

"That was your mom and dad, Julie, and what they wanted was a little girl or boy to be part of their family."

"Your mom and dad were afraid that they could not have any children. I told them just to be patient for sometimes you have to wait a long while for such a blessing.

When your parents finally knew that you were coming, they were as happy as they could be. However, you were a bit late in arriving. That was because when an angel touched a finger to your cheek, she discovered that you were not quite done. That, my darling girl, is why you have a dimple right here on your cheek! It's where the angel touched you!

NO DIMPLES FOR GLORY

When I arrived, my folks already had four children. However, they were all boys. I was their "surprise baby" as they didn't know that I would be a girl. It was about the time when the pink cherry blossoms started to bloom in our garden that the angels made a decision. They decided that since I already weighed ten pounds, I was quite ready to be born. So, without even giving me a single poke, they wrapped me up in a pink flannel blanket and handed me over to their strongest stork for a quick delivery.

SPECIAL DELIVERY!
Whee—What a trip!

TEN POUNDER COMING IN!

People in those days did not know before a baby was born whether it was a boy or a girl, so my Mom shouted *Glory Hallelujah* to express her joy when she learned that their new baby was a girl. (They both loved having four boys, but they had always wanted a girl, too.)

On hearing her shouts, my brothers thought that Glory Hallelujah must be my name, so that's what most everybody started to call me! Before I was born, Morton and Gus had been sleeping in one bedroom while Barney and Henry shared another.

Since Morton was the oldest, he was the first of my brothers to see that we had a problem. He went to Mom and whispered, "I think that we will have to send Glory back. We have no place to put her." Needless to say, Morton was not my favorite brother. Too bad I couldn't talk yet!

Mom told him that I was part of the family now and that the plan was to move to a bigger house where I could have my own room. That room would also double as a playroom for all of us.

Morton thought that he should be the one with a room by himself. "I'm the oldest," he argued. "It's only right that I should have that extra room."
Mom was very firm with her decision. I made a face at Morton, but no one paid any attention.

Two houses later, Morton did get a room of his own, and I was able to convince the other boys that they would have more fun playing in the front room. Mom frowned at that suggestion as she did not like messy houses, but no one else seemed to care.

THE MARCH KIDS

At first, we didn't have too many parties in that house because all five of us kids were born in March. Gus figured out that if we all took turns with our birthday parties that would mean that each of us would only have a birthday party every five years. Now does that sound fair?

We had a family meeting about this and decided that we would all celebrate on the same day in March. Finally, with so many guests invited all at once, we had to take the party outside and pray that it didn't rain.

But sometimes our prayers went unanswered and it did rain. Strangely enough, those days turned out to be the most fun of all!

VACATIONS

Vacations were fun, but it was hard to find a motel for our big family. This one night we saw a motel with a blinking light that said: VACANCY. However, when the manager of the place saw how many of us kids were in the car, he switched off the light.

The next summer we went camping and that worked just fine. I especially liked fishing. What a thrill it was to catch my first fish!

The kids at school liked hearing about that fish I caught. I didn't tell them that my dad said to throw it back in the lake so it could grow bigger for next summer That next summer the fish was so much bigger that it broke my fishing pole, but he still managed to get away!

LAZARUS

The best house we ever lived in was in a small town called Lazarus. When a neighbor boy saw Barney and Henry jumping out of the moving van, he called out: "Welcome to our town—it's the smallest one around!" When Morton, Gus, and I jumped out, he added: "Well, maybe not anymore…"

ALWAYS FIRST

This boy, whose name happened to be Adam, was really friendly and liked to joke a lot. He said that since we came to the town of Lazarus, it wasn't dead any longer. When he laughed, we knew that what he said must be a joke, so we laughed, too.

Adam always liked to be first. He was the first boy in his family; the first kid to get 100% on all his math tests; and the first one in the neighborhood to get a computer.

Even his dog was first in a Smart Pet
Contest. He was the only dog who
could carry a balloon in his mouth
and not pop it. So it was only fitting
that Adam became our very first
friend after we moved to Lazarus.

GETTING LOST

It seems like all of us kids except Morton got lost at one time or another. I know it wasn't my Mom's fault as she was very careful with us. Every time that we would go from one floor to another in a store, she would check on us and count out: "1, 2,3,4,5."

One time she came up with 4, and everyone went wild. Up one aisle and down another, through the dress racks, and under counters, we looked for little Barney.

Since I was just a baby at the time, I wasn't much help. Three-year-olds are not easy to find in a big store, but finally we did see him. He was in the toy department and had a big smile on his face. He didn't look at all frightened about being lost. In fact, he was having fun but said with a gruff little voice:

"Mommy, you have to look after me!"

I got lost just once. It was in a Chinese department store. I was about seven years old and somehow Mom and Dad got absorbed in the sales, for they forgot to count us when we got off the elevator. I went looking for them and managed to get myself lost in the toy department.
(Just like Barney did.) That's where my family found me. This was quite exciting for me, but when I told my friends about it, they acted like it was nothing at all.

HOW IT ALL BEGAN

That's when I decided to add a few things to my story to make it more interesting. This changed everything. Now, everybody was listening carefully to my stories and they all wanted to be my friend.

This is how I told that story with a few "small changes."

Yesterday, my family and I went to Chinatown to shop for Christmas gifts. Just as I was getting off the elevator, I happened to notice how big Henry's feet were. In fact, they were HUGE! Looking up at his face, I see that he had turned into a tall Chinese man with a goatee.

It would seem that I was left behind on the elevator and was now a member of a Chinese family. Frantically, I pressed a button for floor one. When the door opened, I screamed:

"KIDNAPPERS, KIDNAPPERS!"

Two guards asked the Chinese family:

"IS THIS YOUR LITTLE GIRL?"

The Chinese man with the goatee took one look at me and said,

"Are you kidding?"

Just then, after counting to five and only coming up with four, my family showed up, all in a sweat, and claimed me.

That story went over so well with the kids that I decided to retell some of my earlier real life experiences. For instance, I told them about the time that I got trapped in a cubbyhole.

THE CUBBYHOLE
What Really Happened

A friend of mine noticed the door to this cubbyhole in the side of a nearby building. We were both very curious. We pushed the door open and entered. Just about then, a big gust of wind blew the door shut and we were trapped. It was scary in there.

My chilling adventure story ended up getting nothing but yawns out of my listeners, so the next time I told this tale, this is what I did. First, I explained what triggered my memory of the event, and then I told my revised story.

~~~~~~

ADDED TO STORY

One summer, my family took a vacation to Carlsbad Caverns where the tour leader told his group of tourists that soon we would be experiencing

TOTAL DARKNESS!.

He gave us the opportunity of leaving that part of the cave if this would be too frightening for us.
I thought that it would be strange for anyone to have such a reaction. After all, every night we go to bed, we turn off the lights and we end up in the dark.
~~~~~~

When the tour leader went to the light switch he said, "Okay, people, this is your last chance. You now will experience

TOTAL DARKNESS."

As the lights went out, I panicked and had to squeeze my eyes shut to pretend this was why I couldn't see.
I grabbed the railing because I felt like I was going to fall down into the gaping canyon below. Sweat poured from my face and my stomach churned.

Then suddenly, the light went on again, but I was still shaking with fear. Mom hugged me and said that it was alright—that I was just remembering what had happened to me years ago.

REVISED STORY

Bobby Nelson and I were about five years old when this happened. We were playing baseball with some older neighbor kids when Bobby hurt one of them by mistake as he tried to slide into first base. The whole team got mad at us and started to chase us up the street.

Bobby saw that the door to a cubbyhole in this building was open, so he dashed in there to hide. (A cubbyhole is a small space often used for storing things.)

I followed and closed the door. When we saw how dark it was in there, we tried to get out, but the door had locked, and we were trapped.

We felt like crying, but we were both very courageous and did not shed a single tear. In the meantime, our mothers were out looking for us. We began to shout in hopes that they could hear us.

We had been in there about two hours and felt like we were gasping for air. Bobby found an old flashlight, but the battery was dead. Finally, our mothers heard us and tried to get us out, but they couldn't open the door..

They calmed us down by saying they would get the owner of the building to unlock the door.

We waited and waited, but they didn't come back. Suddenly, the frightening sound of a siren broke the silence. We leapt to our feet and started to scream. It sounded like a fire engine was pulling up in front.

THIS PLACE MUST BE ON FIRE!

Then we could hear somebody banging at the lock on the door. When it swung open, we stumbled out and into our mothers' arms. The firemen were there, but there was no fire. They loaded us into an ambulance, gave us oxygen, and sped off to the hospital. We were there for about four hours before we were released.

A NOTE TO JULIE
AND HER FRIENDS

I remember how my classmates liked this story, but I guess I must have been losing my touch. By the time I reached high school, I found out that hardly anyone believed my stories. This was so even though part of each tale was true.

I think that I would have gotten more sympathy from them if I had told them how it really happened.

ARE YOU FOOLED EASILY?

~~~~~~~~~~~~~~~~~~~~~~~~~~~~~~~~~~~

So, for the next two stories, I am going to let you and all the readers test yourselves to see if you are fooled easily. Can you tell if a story is for real or if it is just made up? What are your clues?

Would you be easily fooled if someone told you a "tall tale"?

The answers can be checked later in the book.

Please do not look at the answers until you have read both versions of a story.
~~~~~~~~~~~~~~~~~~~~~~~~~~~~~~~~~~~

THE PLAY
VERSION 1

The second time that I was in first grade, I found out that I had a remarkably good memory. This came in handy for taking tests and remembering people's names. Now that I was older, I could remember what our homework assignment was and hand it in on time.

I even taught myself to read by memorizing whole pages. This was great until we got books with just a few pictures and lots of text to read. After that, I had to go back and memorize each word. Soon I was getting gold stars on every page. My teacher saw how good I was at this so she chose me to play a small part in a play that our class was performing.
After the very first rehearsal, the teacher in charge assigned me the lead role. I played the part of a handicapped girl in a wheelchair.

On stage, I just took one quick look to see where my family was sitting and then I became part of the play. Some of the kids forgot their lines so I prompted them as I had memorized everybody's lines. The play was a great success, and in the weeks that followed, many of the kids in other classes would greet me by saying:

"Hi, little girl, how are you doing today? Where's your wheelchair?"

PROBABLY TRUE?

THE PLAY
VERSION 2

I did not do too well the first time I was in school. It was hard for me to remember what the homework was and to do first grade work. The teacher suggested that maybe I was a bit too young for first grade. My mother was upset, but staying at home did not bother me at all. By the time fall came around again, I was looking forward to starting school.

It was because I got an A in all my subjects that the teacher chose me for the leading role. I had memorized most all of the lines in the play and was able to help those who forgot what they were supposed to say. People recalled my part in the play for years afterward, and because of it, I took acting lessons and found further success in theaters and TV.

PROBABLY TRUE?

Find out on the next page with a star!

THE PLAY:

Version two has the teacher choosing a student to take a lead role based on her getting an A in every subject. The best way would be to see how well the student could act and remember his lines. Version one is more likely the real story.

YIKES!

THE EARTHQUAKE

VERSION 1

I was listening to my fourth grade teacher read a story about Christopher Columbus. It was a warm spring day, and I was half asleep. Suddenly, we felt a strong shake.

The teacher let out a scream and everyone panicked. We knew that it was an earthquake and that it was a bad one. Things started to fall on the floor. Instead of walking out, students began to push and shove.

Some were injured as people tried to get down the stairs. By the time most of us got out, the firemen and police arrived. I looked around and saw that almost the whole city was destroyed.

PROBABLY TRUE?

~~~~~~~~~~~~~~~~~~~~~~~~~~~~~~
~~~~~~~~~~~~~~~~~~~~~~~~~~~~~~

THE EARTHQUAKE
VERSION 2

I was in the fourth grade at school and the teacher was reading a story to us about Christopher Columbus.

When I felt the shake, I thought it was a strong one, and when I looked at the teacher and saw her face turn white, I was scared.

Quickly, she composed herself and told us to get under our desks. In a few minutes, the shaking stopped and we got back to our studies.

PROBABLY TRUE?

When you come to a star, read the answer!

THE EARTHQUAKE:

Since a teacher would want to keep her students safe, she would do her best to stay calm. She could not help that her face turned white, but she needed to speak and act calmly afterward. In the second version of this story, we see the most probable thing that would happen.

SENT TO THE PRINCIPAL

Some of the kids that I gave the earthquake story to must have gotten scared silly (even though as eighth graders they should have known better.) They went straight to Principal Jones and told on me. Then, I got a call to go to the Principal's office.

As soon as I entered the office I knew that I was in deep trouble. She didn't yell at me—she didn't have to. All she did was give me THE LOOK. You know what I mean. Her eyes narrowed and her voice grew husky as she said:

"WHAT ON EARTH DID YOU THINK
YOU WERE DOING?"

I was hanging my head like a sick
puppy,

I hadn't meant to scare anybody by telling that story, but now I feel guilty. My mouth goes dry, and I can't say one word. After hearing what she said, I was expelled for one whole week! Some kids outside the door had been listening, and they were all laughing at me. All I could think of was how I could explain all this to my Dad and Mom.

As it turned out, I didn't have time to explain anything. Dad just pointed to my bedroom door and that was that. After one week of studying at home, I missed school. I missed the social life there (if you can call it that), so I was ready to go back.

~~~~~~~~~~~~~~~~~~~~~~~~~~~~~~
~~~~~~~~~~~~~~~~~~~~~~~~~~~~~~

My return to school was not too spectacular. There was no big WELCOME BACK sign. Even with my baseball team there was no enthusiasm shown for the return of their star player. Even when I hit lots of homeruns and the grownups in the stands were jumping up and down, my team mates were not at all impressed.

PART TWO
TEENAGE YEARS

FIRST DAY IN HIGH SCHOOL

I should have known from past experiences with my classmates that it's hard to guess what they are going to say or do next. One reason for this was that when I first started high school, I only knew about half of the students.

I couldn't believe how many kids were in that freshman class. They didn't even have desks for all of us. We just had chairs with places to write on one arm of the chairs.

This one girl kept whispering to her neighbor so I couldn't hear what the homework was and had to ask someone. That's when once again I ended up being scolded first by the teacher and then by the principal. This time it was for talking in class.

Some who came from my old school saw me there and spread the word that the "Earthquake Kid" just got in trouble again. It took me a year of good behavior to lose that name!

SLAVE DAY

The second day of high school was not too good, either. To welcome us freshmen to high school, the ones in their fourth year there (called seniors) had us act as their slaves for one whole day. They marked us up with red lipstick smearing it all over our faces. This was so that everyone would know that we were freshmen.

Every time we happened to meet on the stairs or in the hallways, we had to bow to them and kneel down. They made us bark like dogs and carry their books. At lunch time, they came around and took out whatever was in our lunch bags that looked good to them. After the last class, we had to sweep the floors and clean the chalkboards in their home room. By the end of the day, I was exhausted. Barney asked me how I liked SLAVE DAY. I just made a face at him.

Bark like a dog!

Little by little, I learned how to get along in school. First of all, you have to find something that you like and that you can do well. (Holidays don't count!) With my four brothers' help, I got pretty good in playing baseball. Other kids noticed this when we started winning a lot of games against other schools.

Being a winner is great, but when you lose, it is no fun at all. I got to be like the fisherman who lies about the size of fish that he catches. I told my teammates that at my last school, we won all kinds of awards because I was GRADE SCHOOL PLAYER OF THE YEAR! I didn't tell them that my award was for showing the most improvement.

Luckily, when I was in my junior year of high school, I had four good friends. I almost lost one by giving her a book called *How to Win Friends and Influence People.*

She thought that I gave her the book because I felt that she was not too popular. (She wasn't popular but neither was I.) Her problem was that she was skinny and mine was that I liked to exaggerate the truth. I thought that exaggeration of the truth would make me more interesting and people would like me more. When I finally decided to be absolutely truthful about things, my friends were impressed until DITCH DAY …

My mother had always told me that I needed to think for myself. I would say, "But, Mom, everyone is doing it."

She would say:

"Makes no difference, Glory. Do what you know is right."

When I got into trouble talking in class, I used as my excuse that "everyone is doing it." Of course, I was the one who got into trouble. So when our class president came up to me and told me how the freshmen were planning a Ditch Day, I figured that I better not go. My reason was:

"Bad luck follows me like my shadow."

Our class president told me that the kids would be furious if even one person stayed behind.

 "Can I count you in, Glory?"

"I guess so," was my answer as I ran up the stairs.

DITCH DAY

On Ditch Day, our part of the school was as quiet as could be. All the freshmen were at a park having fun— all of them except me. I had changed my mind. When the teachers asked me where the other members of my class were, I had no idea what to answer. It wasn't that I did not know where they were. I knew exactly where they were.

If I told the teachers, they would be happy, but the kids would hate me for having ruined their day. If I kept the students' secret and one of them happened to get hurt while they were away from the school, the teachers said I would be responsible.

WHAT WOULD YOU HAVE DONE?

A TALK WITH DAD

After I had made my decision and Ditch Day was over, I had a chat with my dad. He was sitting in his favorite chair watching the news on TV. I asked if he had some time to talk, and he said, "Sure. I'll be glad to get away from the news."

"I have a question."
"And what might that be, Glory?"

"Is telling a lie ever a good thing?"

"I think you know the answer to that, honey. There are times when telling the truth can hurt someone else."

"How can you tell when it's okay?"

"It has to do with kindness, Glory. You should always try to be kind."

"But what if being kind to one person means that you will be unkind to another?"

"Listen to your conscience, dear, and
do what you think is right."
 Dad's advice seemed strange to me
at the time. What he said was:

"Often it is best to say nothing."

"So did I do right on Ditch Day?"

"I didn't ask your mother what you finally decided. Did you think it over carefully and then do what you felt was right?"

"Yes, Dad, I really did."

"Then I trust that you did the right thing. Telling a lie so that you can get out of trouble is a selfish thing to do. It could put the blame on somebody else who is innocent.

Above all, remember this:

Own up to your mistakes."

TEA FOR THE SENIORS

The tea that we juniors gave for the seniors didn't get anybody upset. It was really fun, and there were no problems with it. We had the school's permission to do it and it was great. We juniors dressed like gypsy girls and waited on the seniors. The graduating girls were all dressed in grown-up clothes complete with hats, purses, and long stockings. They looked quite different from the way they dress in school! Some of them even changed their hair styles.

Lovely red and pink roses bordered the inner patio of the school and filled the air with their fragrance. The more talented students accompanied the Gypsy music with their lively dances.

Many girls brought their cameras to the tea and were taking photos to remember the happy occasion.

SENIOR YEAR

Our last year in high school has been really busy. I'm sure that there are a lot more things to learn before we "go out into the real world." All the grownups keep saying that to us as if we are not living out in the real world already. I don't know if college is part of the real world or not, but that is where I am planning on going.

After discovering that exaggerating my true life adventures was not the best way for me to become popular, I did my best to stick to the truth. When my dad spoke in front of the city council to argue in favor of putting in something to block the fast traffic on our street, he won them over.

I almost told the kids at school that later on, my dad became mayor because of that talk. Actually, he never even ran for the office, but I'm sure that he would have won if he had decided to become mayor.

He did such a good job with his speech that we hardly ever hear cars crashing out there anymore. Before, we met all the new neighbors by going out to see the accidents. Now, we hardly meet any of them.

THE PROM

Soon after my return to school after nursing a knee injury, I began to play baseball again. I was making new friends all the time with my team mates, but then came the big news. All the talk around the school was now about the coming Prom. It would be a gala affair with a band and dancing. I had seen proms in movies, and I started to get really nervous about the whole thing.

I had two problems that were bothering me. First of all, I did not know how to dance. (I guess you might call that my biggest problem.)
I bought a book about it with pictures of right and left feet and where to put them. Then, I read that the boy is supposed to do the leading in a dance, and the girl is supposed to follow. I just hoped that whoever got me as a dance partner would have read the same book. Two of us trying to lead could be a disaster.

What would the other kids think?

My second problem is that since I am going to an all-girls school, I don't know any boy that I could ask. In fact, the only boys that I know are my four brothers, and how cool would it look to take your brother to a dance?

I was complaining to my mother about my problems when she came up with a very strange solution. She told me that a cousin of mine who is in the Navy was being transferred to the West Coast. She thought that maybe that could solve my problem.

"You think I should go to the Prom with my cousin? That's almost as bad as going with a brother."

"No, no! I was thinking that we could invite your cousin Ross over for dinner and tell him to bring a friend. Maybe you could go to the Prom with his friend." In doubt, I say,
"What about my cousin?"

"He could go as your friend Eva's date."

This seemed like it might work, so I checked with Eva and she agreed to the plan. When my cousin Ross came to the house with his friend, I was so pleased that I felt like hugging my mother right then and there.

Ross's pal was what we teenagers called a *dreamboat.* That night in my diary I wrote:

Wow!
Ted looks just like a movie star. He has wavy black hair and sparkling blue eyes. I can't wait to hear if he can come to the Prom!

He's a dream boat!

TED

THE BOYFRIEND

We got to visit with Ross about a week before the Prom. It was my Mom who asked my cousin if he would like to go to the Prom with Eva. She told him that my boyfriend had recently left on a short trip but would not be back in time for the Prom. I just about fainted when she said "her boyfriend." What was she talking about? I don't have a boyfriend. Now, she is saying how nice it would be if he could bring along his friend as a date for me!

After Ross left the house to go back to the base, I confronted Mom about the fib that she told. She denied that it was a fib and said that it was just a little white lie meant to solve my problem and make me feel happy.

Even though I knew that my mother was only trying to help me out, I was angry with her for some time.

I had never known her to tell a lie, so this was a shock to me. I began to think about me not telling the exact truth. I enjoyed stretching the truth to make my real life stories more exciting, but how did this affect other people? Are my make-believe tales really lies? In the days that followed, I spent less time trying to figure out the answer to that question and more time wondering if I would be able to keep from stepping on my dance partner's feet!

At this time, my youngest brother, Barney, was 19 years old and offered to show me some new dancing steps. As a toddler, he was the one who got lost in a big store. Come to find out, he was a complete loss on the dance floor as well. He was even worse than me, so I went back to reading my *HOW TO DANCE* book. I think if the school band at the Prom plays waltzes or slow polkas, I will do just fine. Otherwise, I'm a dead duck!

DAY OF RECKONING

The day of reckoning has arrived. The sun is shining and the birds are greeting the world with their sweet melodies, but all I can think of is THE PROM! The very thought of it makes me nervous. Donning my new dress makes me happy at first and then as the skies darken and the time of the dance is imminent, I start to pace up and down waiting for this day of reckoning to begin. I am excited but also scared stiff.

When I hear the doorbell ring, I jump up like a Jack-in-the-Box. I nearly trip over the hem of my long gown as I grab the doorknob. When I see the two boys on the porch, I can't help but show surprise. Somehow or other, I manage to greet them and wave for them to come inside.

WHOOPS!

"Where's Ted?" I ask. As soon as these words left my mouth, my face turned red with embarrassment.

(This was not a polite thing to ask as I didn't want to hurt the new boy's feelings.)

As anybody could see, this boy was not Ted. The boy at the door was blond with blue eyes and seemed very, very shy. I took a quick look at Eva and was glad to see that she was shaking hands with Ross, and the two were already chatting away.

I   tried to talk with the new boy but was having no luck at all. My parents and four brothers had been standing by, and after listening in for a while, my Dad handed his car keys to Cousin Ross. Then, he gave some instructions: "Be sure to drive slowly out there and be back by midnight."

At that moment, I felt just like Cinderella with my fancy long dress and *curfew. When we got out to the car, it became quite evident that none of us had been on a date before.

 No sooner had Ross slid in behind the steering wheel than the new boy, James, hopped in beside him.

Now, somehow or other, I knew that this was not right. I had seen enough movies to spot this right off. With my friendly voice, I called out:

"Hey, James, why don't you let Ava sit there alongside her date?"

James did as he was told and off we went for the Prom.

*curfew: a time limit

One more little thing happened on the way. Cousin Ross had not understood my father's directions. He thought that he was supposed to do more than just go slowly. He thought that he was supposed to stop at the end of each block, and that is exactly what he did.

One car behind us almost ran into us but stopped in time. The driver was furious and began to honk his horn loud and long. After that, Ross asked if it would be alright if he just went slowly instead of stopping at each corner. We all nodded our heads in relief.

AT THE PROM

I felt like I was a princess going to my first ball. The building was decorated with fresh roses. Many of the girls, in their pretty gowns, were already dancing. Most of the handsome young men were dressed in suits and ties. The rest of the people sat along the sides of the dance floor listening to the lively music and watching their friends swirl by.

We had been told by our teachers that it would be a special treat for them if we introduced our dates to them when we come to the ball. In those days, such a request was not just a suggestion. It was more like a command.

Lining up with the other students, we waited our turn. None of the other fellows were in the service except for one, and he, too, was wearing civilian clothes.

It was all very exciting, and I was wondering if the Prom would be anything like I had seen in the movies. I was dreaming about how it would be as we walked in.

THIS IS HOW I HOPED IT MIGHT BE.

THIS IS HOW IT WAS…

Dancing seemed to be painful for James Philip. First, he stepped on my toes and then I stepped on his. Pretty soon, we started stepping on other people's toes, and that was it. We gave it all up and spent most of the evening sitting on a bench.

ONE OF OUR "VICTIMS"

AFTER THE PROM

Thankfully, Eva was absent from school the day after the Prom. The kids were all busy talking about the dance and teasing people who didn't know too much about *gala affairs.* I was glad when the school bell rang, and I could hide out in English class.

The teacher gave us an interesting assignment: The title would be *THE PROM.* I raised my hand and asked,

"Does the story have to be real or can it be make-believe?"

A few of the kids giggled at this point and started to whisper to each other. The teacher stopped all this by letting us know that the story did not have to be true. I was so glad that she said this. If the story is accepted as not being true, how can it hurt a person's feelings? Well, I was just about to find out.

ONE LAST QUESTION

We were getting ready to leave for our next class when the teacher had one more thing to say.

"Well, it looked like most everyone was having a good time dancing at the Prom. Miss Glory, tell us where did you pick up those sailors?"

The whole class (except for me) began to laugh. I was speechless.

There was no way that I was going to let those girls know that one of the sailors was my cousin. I would rather have them think I was picking up someone off the street just so I would have a date for the Prom. I sank down in my seat and fiddled with some papers. I could hardly wait for the bell to ring.

When I got home, I didn't tell anyone what had happened at school. I decided to sit right down and get started with my story about the Prom. It would be make-believe, alright, but have enough truth in it to get the attention of my classmates

The following day when I walked into my English class, some of the kids began to snicker and laugh. I almost lost courage at this point, but when the teacher came in, I was determined to see this thing through.

When she asked for our homework, I was one of the first to turn in my work. I was really eager to share!

MY NOTE TO THE TEACHER

Here is the note that I am putting on top of my assignment.

English assignment by Glory Hallelujah Warren

NOTE:

This is **not** a true story. The people are **not** real, either. I drew two of the pictures.

Glory

THE PROM

Written by Glory Hallelujah Warren

Long ago and far away, a mighty king decided that his people should be rewarded for their service to him. He would do this by giving them fine schools throughout the land. One of these fine schools was in the province called HAPPY VALLEY. This is where the young Prince Ted lived.

Prince Ted wanted to come to the Prom, but he didn't want anyone to recognize him. His friend James suggested that he should go in disguise. Prince Ted chose a blond wig and wore James' glasses. He looked very nice but not at all like himself.

The prince had James wear a black wig to match Prince Ted's real hair. Even the King did not recognize that the black-haired boy was not his son.

The only trouble was that James now had to wander about with no glasses at all. Consequently, he kept bumping into empty chairs and saying, "Excuse me, miss!"

The girls at the Prom still thought that James was the prince and that he was just joking with them. Did they also dance with the quiet young man with blond hair and glasses? No, they went up to James and asked him to sign up to dance with them.

They were so happy when the fake prince smiled at them. They thought he was truly the real prince and someday one of them might even become his princess!

Only one girl paid any attention to the quiet boy sitting on the bench. It really didn't matter to her that he was not a good dancer. She had no idea that he was the Prince, but she did know that they were destined to be the best of friends.

THE END

After the teacher read my story, she told the class that it was the best of all the ones she had read and that she especially liked the plot. According to her, it would make a nice short story for young children.

"However," she said, "I am not going to tell you who the author is—you will just have to guess."

After she said this, almost all of the girls turned around and looked at me. I guess they got the message and figured out who wrote that story.

As for my folks, they will just think that it is another fairy tale of mine and has nothing to do with real life.

SWIM PARTY

Our last big event was when we had a swim party at a nearby lake resort.

I enjoyed splashing around in the lake although I did not know how to swim.

I thought I might get a nice tan which was so popular then, but I just ended up with a terrible sunburn.

The party itself was a lot of fun, but I missed having my best friend there. She had moved to Arizona a few months before, and I really missed her.

We kept in touch by writing letters to each other. At first, I was surprised to hear that she was having fun there with her *best friend*. I learned that *she* had known this "best friend" for years before she ever came to California.

That's when I learned that even though someone may be your best friend doesn't mean that you are theirs! However, we were both lucky to have her as a close friend.

It was just too bad that there were not two of them!

GRADUATION

I could hardly get fitted for my graduation robe because of my bad sunburn from the swim party.

After that ordeal, we practiced singing our own special words to the tune of *I'M ALWAYS CHASING RAINBOWS*. I never thought that was a sad song until we stood up on the stage stairs with tears in our eyes and sang our goodbyes to high school days. But when we reached the end of the song, we tossed our mortar boards high into the air and could only cheer for the days yet to come!

Here you see a picture of me when I was dreaming of my future. Can you guess which   part of my dream came true? Look below my "hat" on the page that follows.

Glory H. Philip